One snowy day

Diana Murray
Diana Toledano

sourcebooks
jabberwocky

**For Danny, Kate, Jane, and
snow-loving puppies everywhere.**
—Diana M.

**To Steve, who loves the snow and who will
(eventually) convince me to rescue a dog.**
—Diana T.

Text © 2018 by Diana Murray
Cover and internal art © 2018 by Diana Toledano
Cover and internal design © 2018 by Sourcebooks, Inc.

Sourcebooks and the colophon are registered trademarks of Sourcebooks, Inc.

The illustrations were created using mixed media on paper and on the computer.

Published by Sourcebooks Jabberwocky, an imprint of Sourcebooks, Inc.
P.O. Box 4410, Naperville, Illinois 60567-4410
(630) 961-3900
Fax: (630) 961-2168
sourcebooks.com

Library of Congress Cataloging-in-Publication data is on file with the publisher.

Source of Production: Shenzhen Wing King Tong Paper Products Co. Ltd., Shenzhen, Guangdong Province, China
Date of Production: June 2018
Run Number: 5012533

Printed and bound in China.
WKT 10 9 8 7 6 5 4 3 2 1

Spinning and twirling,
they float to the ground—
millions of snowflakes
not making a sound.

The house is all quiet
and still nearly dark,
when **one** playful puppy
leaps up with a bark!

TWO sleepy children
are soon out of bed,

yawning and stretching, then patting his head.

The snow coats the treetops
and covers the grass

as **three** happy faces
peer out through the glass.

Some cheering and dancing,
a quick bite to eat,

then out come **four** snow boots
for **four** stomping feet.

Dragging a sled
on a blanket of snow,
passing **five** pine trees
with branches hung low.

Behind the old school,

where the icy creek bends,

there are **six** boys and girls

waving down to their friends.

Seven sleds glide
as **one** dog wags his tail.

They speed down the hill, leaving **eight** curvy trails.

Falling back—whoosh!—

in a snow bank below,

carving **nine** snow angels,
swishing in snow.

Packing and piling

a frosty white batch—

ten perfect snowballs
for Puppy to catch!

Placing **nine** buttons

in neat little rows,

then **eight** chase a bandit...
"Hey, give back that nose!"

With **seven** scarves blowing,

they laugh as they run.

They can't catch that puppy,
but trying is fun!

Six silver lampposts,
five birds in the sky,
and **four** paws slip-sliding
as friends wave good-bye.

Three faces warmed by the fire, so cozy.

Two cups of cocoa make cheeks nice and rosy.

And **one** sleepy puppy
is starting to doze,

snuggled up tight

with a bright carrot nose.

While spinning and twirling,

so fluffy and light,

millions of snowflakes...

fall all through the night.